Mine to Cherish

Veteran K9 Team

Book 1

Kameron Claire

Snuggle Whore Press, LLC

Editor: Shay M Williams

Covers by SWP Covers

!! Formerly Titled: Dog Tags !!

Dedication

This series is dedicated to every individual
who signs a blank check on their ass
by enlisting in the Armed Forces
to serve their country—and to the
loved ones who support them back home.

We are Witty, Wicked & Wild wherever we go!

VETERAN
K9
TEAM
REPORTING
FOR DUTY

Chapter 1
Cher

"You know we're restricted to garrison the night before we deploy." I padlock the top of my duffle bag and stuff my uniform into my backpack. This is my second deployment in the six years of serving full time in the reserves, which means I'm military 24/7 like active duty, but assigned locally and not subject to being moved per the whims of the US government.

Colorado is my home.

Always has been.

Always will be.

Mari, my best friend since junior high and fellow staff sergeant in the Army Reserves, flashes me a smile that spells pure trouble. "They'll never know we're missing."

"How do you figure?" I hoist my sack over my shoulder and walk out the front door, dumping it in the back of her Jeep. I'm fine with staying at the pre-deployment barracks tonight considering I took Sookie, my eight-month-old Husky, to the Veteran K9 Center a few hours ago, and the house is empty without her.

She'll be kenneled at their facility for the next six months, which absolutely breaks my heart.

She'll also have daily play time, training sessions and human interaction sixteen hours a day, which is better attention than I give her now.

Simply put, it is the best place near Spring City for a military member to leave their dog while away on a long-term deployment, training exercise, or school. Veterans built it for military members.

Of course, if I was married, she'd stay home with my spouse and kids. As it is, I haven't had a date in forever, much less a boyfriend serious enough to entrust my dog to. If I had family nearby, I would ask them to watch her, but my parents retired to Florida two years ago and I can't force my fluffy, snow-loving, Husky to survive a summer in the Florida heat.

She'd be bald by the time I came back.

I know I have nothing to worry about. The trainers at the VKC are the absolute best. They will take excellent care of Sookie, and she'll be a better trained dog by the time I get back.

Still, I'm going to miss her furry face.

Mari climbs her short, curvy ass into the driver's seat of her lifted Jeep. "Because Chris is on duty tonight, nine pm to nine am, and he's already marked us as present and accounted for."

"Shut up." I shake my head and hop into the

passenger seat, my long legs making it easy. "You did not pay off the door guard for a night of debauchery."

Mari holds up her hands. "No money exchanged hands. He owes me for setting him up with Jennie a couple of months ago."

I shake my head and chuckle. "Girl, if we get caught, we'll catch hell."

"We are two of five women going on this deployment and the only ones who are single. We need a night out to let off steam before we are stuck in testosterone hell for the next six months." Mari smiles and hands me two condom foils as if sex is a given, which is crazy considering I haven't been laid in a long time. "Trust me."

By eight pm, Mari and I are at the Last Stand drinking beer, playing pool, and listening to music. This is a country-style bar down Highway 24 just outside of Spring City heading toward the VKC, which of course makes me think of Sookie. It's not too far from my place, but far enough on a Sunday night that I'm ninety percent confident no one from our unit will stumble in.

Not one hundred percent, because even with seven hundred and fifty thousand people in Spring City, it's still a remarkably small town where the six degrees of separation are more like four and a half.

Which means I'm cautiously watching the door, and

clock him the moment he walks in. I track him from the corner of my eye as he orders a beer and turns his body to face the table. He watches for a couple of minutes with blatant interest, so I'm not surprised when he walks up and puts his quarters down, flashing me a panty-melting grin. "Can I play the winner?"

"That would be me." I smile wolfishly at the same time I put the eight ball in the corner pocket.

"Dammit." Mari hands him her cue and grabs a set of quarters. "I hope you enjoy getting spanked by a woman."

"I prefer to do the spanking, but I'll entertain it with the right woman." He answers her, but his eyes are on me.

I let my gaze trail down his body, taking in all six foot-three inches of him. He's got broad shoulders, a wide chest and thick thighs hugged by a pair of well-worn jeans. He's wearing weathered combat boots—desert issue—and a T-shirt that hugs his bulging biceps perfectly. I'd guess he's on active duty if it wasn't for the dark beard and long hair hanging in his eyes.

Probably ex-military—like so many others in this town.

My eyes settle on his lips, which are curled into a knowing smile as I inventory every sexy detail about him, the realization that I will never see this man again tickling the back of my brain.

Six months in the desert running the armory.

Twelve hours a day, seven days a week, one hundred and eighty days straight.

My life is about to be a monotonous blur—Groundhog Day over and over again.

Why shouldn't I take this man to my bed tonight and give myself a fantasy to replay over the next six months?

"Care to make a wager?" I lean across the pool table, making sure to flash plenty of cleavage while lining up the break.

His green-gray eyes lock onto my breasts as he blatantly picks up every nanobyte of sexual energy I'm throwing his way. "What did you have in mind?"

"What are you willing to lose?"

"To you?" His hot gaze caresses me. "A lot."

I glance over his shoulder and lock eyes with Mari, who is at the bar watching us, and flash her two fingers. She nods with a wicked smile and turns to the bartender, Tess, ordering us shots of Jameson and beer chasers.

"How about a hundred bucks?" I raise my brow.

He narrows his eyes. "I smell a shark."

I shrug. "If it's too rich for your blood—"

"Okay." He pulls a money clip out of his back pocket and tosses a hundred-dollar bill onto the green felt.

My jaw drops. "I was kidding."

"Too rich for your blood?"

"No, but I don't have a hundred bucks on me right now."

"Do you want to write me an IOU?"

I chuckle. "No."

He tilts his head and looks at me, drinking me in and getting his fill. "I tell you what. If you win, I'll give you this crisp one-hundred-dollar bill. But if I win—"

"What do you get?" Cocking my hip, I arch my brow and dare him to say what we are both thinking.

"A kiss."

That's not what I was expecting. "Just a kiss?"

"One simple kiss. Anything more and we'd be playing for a helluva lot more money."

"You assume it would be worth the price?"

"I have no doubts it would be worth my kingdom and more—" he smiles sheepishly "—if I had a kingdom to lose."

"One kiss?"

He nods.

"You're on." Grinning, I lean forward, wiggle my ass and line up my break, sinking three solids and one stripe.

He stands back and watches as I nearly run the table, putting five of the seven solids in the hole before giving him a turn. Taking a deep swig of his beer, he smiles and nods, accepting a shot glass from Mari. The three of us clink our glasses and shoot back one and then a second Jameson.

I swear, Mari is the best wingwoman and the worst influence. Both devil and angel rolled into one curvy, dark beauty.

She's been the one getting me in trouble since our junior year in high school, and I love her for it.

"Are you trying to get me drunk so I'll lose?" Sexy man says.

I don't know his name and I don't feel the need to ask, especially since I have no intention of telling him my name or the fact that I'm out of here in the morning.

"You're going to lose drunk or sober." I grin.

"Am I?" He sets his beer down and chalks his cue before turning to the table and sinking four stripes in two shots.

"Shit," I mutter.

"Nervous?" Smiling, he lines up his next shot and puts it in the hole.

"And you called me a shark."

"You're the one who suggested a hundred bucks." He sinks the next two shots and is left with only the eight ball, which is cradled by the center pocket. There's no way he's going to miss. "How about we do the best two out of three?"

I tilt back my beer and drain it of its contents. "You don't want to beat me and collect your kiss right away?"

He sinks the eight ball and tosses the triangle on the felt before walking up behind me and placing his mouth near my ear. "Anticipation is part of the fun, don't you think?"

I can't help myself. I lean back and turn my face slightly to find his mouth so close I could claim his lips right now if I wanted to. "Two out of three?"

"Rack 'em." He growls and slides his hand down my hip, lightly smacking my ass.

We play another game, and this time I win, even though I'm pretty sure he let me. He racks the third game and I break, warmth from the whiskey running through my veins. This man is pure sex, and I can't wait to kiss him. It's not within me to lose graciously—even if the terms of the wager benefit me as much as they do him—so I can't give up without a fight.

I sink three stripes and then one more before turning the table over to him. Glancing around the bar, I find Mari talking to a guy at the jukebox while playing a variety of music, her hips moving in a hypnotic way that even I find enticing.

Wondering if I can use the art of seduction to steal my opponent's concentration and win the last game, I dance with my pool cue at the edge of the table and swing my hips. I mean, let's face it. I'm going to be kissing him tonight regardless of whether or not I lose the bet. So why lose?

He arches his brow and watches me. "Are you trying to distract me?"

"That depends." I dip low with purpose. "Is it working?"

With a sexy smirk, he keeps his eye on me while sinking two more solids. "Something tells me you're a distraction no matter what you're doing, darlin'."

Then he diverts his attention back to the game and sweeps the felt in the next five shots, the eight ball traveling painfully slow across the green. I sigh and toss my cue on the table, giving up the seduction by placing my hands on my hips. "I guess you win."

"I guess I do." He tosses his cue next to mine and walks to me, sliding his hand over my hip. "Come dance with me."

His fingers slide to my lower back and curl into my belt loops as he escorts me to the small dance floor where

Mari is swaying back and forth with her beau for the evening. Sexy Man swings me into his arms, pulling me flush against his hard body, and I'm instantly wet and wanting more.

"Should I take my winnings now or see if I can turn you on before claiming my kiss?" His voice is rich and gruff, as if the anticipation is finally getting to him too.

I lick my lips and look up through my lashes at him. "I'm already turned on."

"Are you?" He lowers his mouth to my ear and nuzzles my neck, causing my insides to turn into molten goo. "How turned on?"

I slide my fingers into his hair, scraping my nails against his scalp. "Take me to your place and find out."

"I'll close our tab," he says without preamble.

"I'll let my friend know I'm leaving."

He wraps a lock of my hair around his finger and tilts my chin up, claiming my lips in a way that sends tingles straight to my pussy. "I'll wait for you at the front door."

I watch him walk to the bar before I turn and tap Mari on the shoulder, her head resting on the jukebox guy's chest. "Sorry to interrupt, but I need thirty seconds."

The guy nods and tilts his head to the jukebox. "I'll pick the next couple of songs."

"What's going on with the hottie?" Mari glances between me and Sexy Man, who is paying our tab at the bar.

"I'm going home with him. How do I do this and not get court-martialed in the morning?"

Mari grins. "Be back at the barracks by five a.m. I'll let Chris know to sneak you in."

"Okay."

"But I want blow-by-blow details tomorrow on the flight over there." Mari giggles.

I glance over my shoulder at the man moving from the bar to the front door, his green-gray eyes on me. "Blow-by-blow sounds right."

VETERAN
K9
TEAM
REPORTING
FOR DUTY

Chapter 2
Vale

I did not expect my first night in Spring City to end like this, but this redhead is the hottest woman I've ever met. I walked into the Last Stand to have a drink, maybe grab a burger or a container of hot wings to go and then go back to my new place to contemplate what furniture I need to buy over the next couple of months to make this new house my home, or bachelor pad, as Janey pointed out yesterday.

I came to Spring City with nothing besides a couple of trash bags full of clothing and my computer.

My buddy Kemp—a guy I've known since joining the Army fourteen years ago—gave me the bed out of his spare room until I could buy my furniture. Earlier tonight, I was wondering why I didn't choose to stay with him until I had the basic necessities.

Now, I know.

I swing open the passenger door of my truck, and she approaches like a tigress who'd finally been freed from her cage. She backs me up against the door—uses the running board to pull herself up—and wraps her arms around my neck to climb me like a tree.

Without hesitation, I slide my hands under her ass and hold her up, kissing her with the same need, same desire, same desperation. Fuck, I haven't felt this kind of incessant need to drive myself deep into a woman in over a year.

Maybe ever?

"How far to your place?" She pants while grinding her jean-clad pussy against my cock.

"Three miles."

"Let's go."

I set her into the passenger seat and am in the driver's seat cranking the engine in two point five seconds, practically peeling out of the parking lot of the roadside bar and heading out of Spring City toward the VKC. It's a local country bar—reportedly hopping on Friday and Saturday nights—and a favorite amongst my team members because it is on the way back into town from the center where we all work.

She perches beside me in her seat with one hand on my thigh, creeping higher by the second. Her lips are on my neck and it takes everything within me to keep my truck centered on the residential street. I have one hand wrapped around the steering wheel, the other between her jean-clad thighs to palm her round ass when I finally roll to a stop in my driveway. She uses the perceived safety of the engaged brakes to climb onto my lap, straddling my thighs and claiming my lips.

Fuck, this woman is amazing. I've never had a female this beautiful damn near devour me. You'd think my ex-wife would've felt this way about me at one time or another, but no.

Not like this.

No one has ever been with me like this.

This is new and I suspect I'm going to be addicted to the powerful feeling.

Hell, I'm already hooked on her.

Popping open my door, I somehow slide out with her wrapped around me and carry her through my front door and straight to the bedroom, falling to the bare bones mattress and box spring.

Thank god Kemp loaned this set to me. I owe that man big time.

She grins and yanks at the hem of my T-shirt. "Off. Now."

"Fuck, you are a wildcat."

"And you are too sexy for your own good." She works the buttons of her jeans, kicking her feet to push the denim down her long, muscular legs.

I toss my T-shirt toward the corner and then help her pull her shirt over her head.

"Oh, fuck me." I groan, dropping my face between her plump breasts.

She chuckles. "Are you a breast or ass man?"

"With you? I'm an everything man."

"Mmmm. Good answer. Now get your pants off." She pulls on my belt and my mind goes blank. My singular focus is getting naked—with her. Foreplay, well... I guess that is what we've been doing for the last hour.

I stand up and drop my pants, kicking them and my shoes off in a solid heap. My thoroughly neglected cock juts from my hips and this amazing woman does the best thing a man with a recently trampled ego like mine could —she sucks in her breath, wraps her fingers around me and then licks her lips. "Wow."

I brush her lush red hair back from her face. "I'm glad you think so."

She rolls to her knees and parts her plump lips, taking me as deep as she can go. My eyes roll back into my head as I lose myself to the pleasure. It's been so goddamn long and I pray I don't embarrass myself. I let this vixen work me until I'm on the edge, then I push her to her back and dive face first between her legs. Yanking her panties off, I replace the cotton barrier with my tongue. Sweet and tangy arousal coats my tastebuds instantly. I groan, plunging deep inside her channel before sucking her engorged clit against my teeth.

"Oh god." She bucks her hips, riding my mouth and demanding her pleasure. "Just like that. Don't stop."

My vixen explodes underneath me, her fingers pulling on chunks of my hair as a full body orgasm runs through her perfect body.

Now, this is something to become addicted to.

Getting her off, the unbridled display of passion and pleasure she wears so easily—absolutely intoxicating.

My ego climbs out of the catacombs it went to die in over a year ago, and my dick throbs between my legs when I suddenly remember—I don't have any condoms. I barely have a toothbrush and a shaving kit with me.

As if reading my mind, she pants, "Condoms. In my front pocket."

Wordlessly, I pull myself off her and grab her jeans. She retrieves two foil wrappers and tosses the denim to the side again.

With veiled desperation, she rips one packet open and rolls the lubricated barrier down onto my erection. Like all guys, I fucking hate these things, but considering it's been well over a year since I've had sex, I'm thankful for the staying power the damned prophylactic will give me. Even with the rubber, slipping into her feels like heaven. I groan and rest my face in the crook of her neck as my cock pulses.

Sinfully Sexy digs her nails into my ass cheeks as she locks her heels behind my lower back.

"Please fuck me good," she whimpers as I slowly move my hips.

It hasn't escaped my notice that I don't know her name. But at this point, while I'm cock-deep inside her, it feels insulting to ask. I'll suss it out in the morning, while we're out to breakfast and I learn how she takes her coffee.

I pull her legs up higher and drive deeper with every stroke, encouraged by her moans. My ex-wife cheating on me dealt a huge blow to my self-esteem, but with this gorgeous woman underneath me, I realize it was the years of subpar sex and her lack of desire that really shredded my ego.

It doesn't take long for me to know what this vixen likes and what she loves. She's so expressive—every moan, gasp and *fuck yes* telling me how to please her. I'm close to coming when her cunt clamps down, nails dig into my shoulders and a scream rips from her throat. She pulls me over the edge with her—and I come harder than I have in years.

VETERAN
K9
TEAM
REPORTING
FOR DUTY

Chapter 3
Vale

I wake up naked and alone with my cock at half-mast, memories of sinking into my mystery woman's hot, wet body at the forefront of my mind.

Where is she?

Bathroom?

Kitchen?

I roll out of bed and grab my boxer shorts off the ground, noticing that none of her clothes are intermingled with mine—besides her underwear hidden precariously under my jeans.

Hmmm.

"Hello?" I call, sliding on my shorts and walking down the hall into the kitchen.

No one.

Nothing.

Not even a note with a name and number—not that I have a pad of paper or a pen for her to leave it on.

Fuck.

I flop back into bed. The motion causes a puff of her jasmine perfume to waft up from my pillow. My dick instantly goes from semi- to fully hard with her scent in my nostrils, visions of her riding me before we passed out replaying in vivid detail through my mind.

My phone beeps with a text message, pulling me out of my head and away from my aching cock.

> Janey: Sorry for hitting you up so early. We have an eight-month-old Husky-Malamute who isn't doing well at the center. Her owner ships out today for six months and the dog has been a wreck all night. Think you can handle your first client?

I'm an Army veteran and a K9 trainer, and I specialize in intelligent breeds that are prone to destroying things when not properly engaged. After tearing my ACL and MCL during a training accident, the Army medically retired me, but it wasn't until my wife asked for a divorce six months ago—she had shacked up with another soldier and he popped hot on orders—that my buddy Kemp invited me to join him and other trainers at the Veteran K9 Center outside of Spring City, Colorado.

This town has a large military presence and in the early two-thousands when deployments to Afghanistan, Iraq and other Middle Eastern locales were plentiful, my new boss and fellow ex-soldier, Janey LaVey, saw a need to assist military members with no family by providing affordable and dependable animal care. Too many military members were needlessly re-homing or losing their furry four-legged babies while serving their country and —let's face it—worrying about what's going on back home is a stress service members don't need.

> I'm up. Let me take a shower and get some coffee in me and then I'll swing by the center for a meet and greet. If the dog takes to me, I'll bring her home.

> Great. Thanks. I don't want to alert the owner, especially since they will be on a plane in the next few hours. See you soon.

There are five of us at the center now that I've arrived in town. We're all veterans, all ex-K9 handlers—Janey, Kemp, Barron, Linc, and now me. Janey, Kemp, and I went through AIT together after boot camp and have been friends ever since. Our first duty assignment was in Georgia, where we were assigned to the 75th Rangers Battalion. We reported to SFC Barron Theroux who is now retired, divorced and—in his words—living a low-stress bachelor life. Linc, who is a good five or six years younger than me, worked for Kemp and me at one time or another.

Even though we all have years of K9 training experience, Janey is the one with the big plans and even bigger dreams. It's her goal to bring six of us on to round out the team, but we'll have to wait for Karden and Saint to separate from the military in the next year to join us.

After a quick shower and a coffee shack run, I walk into the office to be greeted by a mournful ruckus coming from the kennels. I raise my brow in Janey's direction. "What in fresh hell is that?"

"That's a spoiled dog missing her mommy."

"A female's dog?"

Janey sighs and hands me a folder full of papers, a leash and a collar. "Big cage at the end of row two. You can't miss her. Name is Sookie."

S ix Months Later...
Arrrraaauuuooowwww.

I peel open my eyelids and come face to face with dog lips. "What do you two want?"

Arrrraaauuuuooooowwww. Sookie rears back and smacks me across the face with her wet snout while, at the same time, my dog Strijker—the one I adopted four months ago—jumps on the bed.

"It's like you know your momma will be home any day now." I wipe my face and lean up on my elbow. Sookie takes this as an invitation to bounce around in a circle, her chest pressed against the floor, her rear end wagging high in the air. "You miss her, huh?"

She bounces forward and sneak-attacks me with a tongue up my cheek before making a mad dash for her food bowl, which I will have to pack up later today. Strijker leaps off the bed and chases after her, leaving me alone to contemplate my day. Not that I have long.

If I don't get my ass out of bed, they will be back with a lot more mouthy energy to demand their morning kibble.

In the last six months, Sookie and I have done a lot of training and she's socialized often with other dogs, living with me and Strijker most of the last few months. I have to admit, I'm more attached to her than I should be. She's a good dog—smart, loving and playful—and gets along beautifully with my boy.

It will be an adjustment for Strijker and me once she's gone, but we'll get through it.

I don't talk to the owners of the dogs I train unless I'm actively training their humans too. Kennel dogs are something Janey handles. She keeps up correspondence with the owners while they are deployed. I provide weekly reports with pictures and leave the rest of the interaction with her.

With the dogs fed, I take care of my morning business before grabbing a travel mug of coffee and a freshly nuked breakfast burrito. Then I shuttle the fur-kids into my truck and hit the road.

Sookie will stay the next few nights at the center to wait for her momma to come get her. And because I can't stand the idea of her being alone in a kennel at night, I'll leave Strijker behind while I take some time off and hit the summer trails on my mountain bike.

Six months of living in Colorado and I've yet to climb a mountain or sleep under the stars.

Seems almost criminal.

"So, you're finally taking a couple of days off?" Kemp

rubs Strijker and Sookie's heads, sneaking both of them a small treat.

"Yeah, I'll be staying near Crested Butte."

"Nice. Your first Colorado mountain vacation." Kemp looks around the office for anyone within earshot, and I know he's about to say something inappropriate. He's always been the bad idea fairy sitting on my shoulder. "Have fun. Find a girl. Get laid."

"What makes you think I need to get laid?" I frown.

"Dude." Kemp arches his brow in challenge. "Are you still pining over your one-night stand from six months ago?"

"She was awesome." I shrug. "What can I say?"

"Yeah, and she ghosted you. You've been hanging out at the Last Stand for months and she's never once walked through the door. Neither has her friend. Find yourself another woman to warm your bed, man." Kemp runs his hand down his long, full beard and shakes his head. "Nora fucked you up, buddy, and I hate seeing you like this."

Nora is my ex-wife.

Kemp knew her and the guy she left me for.

And the dog she took on her way out the door.

He knows about all of it.

"I'll think about it," I grumble.

"Good. I'll take care of the kids while you're gone."

I kneel and cradle Sookie's head. "I'll miss you, girl, but hopefully your momma will bring you in for play dates once in a while."

She jumps up on her back legs and presses the top of

her head against my chest. Strijker, not to be outdone, jumps up clumsily and knocks her off me, the two puppies instantly at play in the small office. Kemp sighs and stands, his better-trained Shepherd, Krieger, awaiting a command. "I'll take them to the pit to burn off some of this energy."

"Thanks." I grab a few things out of my desk and wait until Kemp and the dogs are outside before leaving.

The drive into the mountains is solitary and peaceful. I'm listening to an audiobook, more self-help mumbo-jumbo because Kemp isn't wrong about how fucked up I was when Nora left. She'd blindsided me, which was as much my fault as it was hers. I wasn't present in our relationship, and after years of deploying, maybe I took Nora for granted.

Not that it excuses her cheating on me.

Or stealing all my shit and my dog.

But that was almost a year ago and I've been working on myself the entire time—long before a fiery redhead rocked my world. She was perfect—exactly the kind of woman I like.

Confident, smart and beautiful.

And the sex? Good god, my cock rouses just thinking about it.

I know next to nothing about her—her name, for instance—but I feel like we connected on a different level.

The attraction was there.

The playfulness—there.

The soul-deep knowledge that there could have been more to us—if only we had time.

Hell, maybe Kemp is right?

I'm all wrapped up in a woman who may be nothing like the femme fatale I built in my mind. For all I know, she could be another Nora.

Fuck—she could be married and I would never know the difference.

Damn, that sucks to think about. I have no desire to be a guy that does to another guy what was done to me. Not that any of it matters now. After six months, it's obvious I'm never going to see her again, which sucks because no other woman has grabbed my attention since that night. Sure, attractive women hit on me occasionally, but none of them have that spark that calls to me on a primal level.

Call me a dumbass—being a simple man who thinks with nothing more than his dick would be so much easier —but I want something more meaningful than sex. I'm looking for an instant connection where I know by looking across the room that she's the one I want. That's what it was like with my fiery redhead. I knew the moment I walked into the bar she was going to be mine.

Of course, I shouldn't have taken her home that night. I guess I can't be surprised she didn't take me seriously. Married or not, I approached her like a one-night stand.

No wonder she left before I could take her on a real date—or ask her name.

I pull into the campground, park my truck in my

designated spot, and unpack my gear. After moving here, I retrofitted my truck with a tent over the eight-foot bed. It's perfect for camping, and big enough for the next time when I have Strijker with me. Not sure how I'll deal with him and mountain biking, but he'll be a perfect companion for fishing and hiking.

Damn, I miss the dogs already. Going home on Tuesday is not going to be the same with Sookie no longer part of the family. That's the only danger with fostering dogs while their owners are deployed. Six months is a lot of time to connect to these animals, and breaking said bond is going to suck every time.

For the next several hours, I ride hard before taking a refreshing dip in a small river off of the lake. I haven't seen another person all day, but that night I fall asleep listening to the sounds of the narrator talk about emotional availability and letting go of the past.

VETERAN
K9
TEAM
REPORTING
FOR DUTY

Chapter 4
Cher

I wake to my ringing phone. It takes me a minute to remember where I am while wrapped comfortably in my fluffy blankets and fresh linens. There is something about the creature comforts of home that make you drunk without a sip of alcohol.

I pat the bed, but the spot I expect to find my dog sleeping in is empty. Sitting up, I ignore my phone and call out, "Sookie?"

They told me it could be days or weeks before she adjusts back into our routine. Luckily, I have the next three weeks off and plan to spend every minute with my fluffy girl. I crawl out of bed, naked, for the first time in six months. That's the thing about being deployed. Even when you think you're alone, you're not.

Not really.

Your only naked time is in the shower and even there you have to wear shower shoes.

Communal living at its finest.

Throwing on a pair of shorts and a tank top, I snag my phone off the nightstand and walk through the house, calling for my girl. "Sookie?"

My phone rings again and I answer it without looking, at the same time finding my back door ajar. "Hello?"

"Do you own a Husky mix named Sookie?" A male's voice barks, deep with annoyance.

"I do. Where is she?"

"She's at my house. I came home this morning to find her sleeping on the back porch. I understand you've been gone a long time, but as the owner of a breed who has a natural tendency to roam, you have to take better care of her."

I'm appalled by the tongue-lashing I'm receiving from a total stranger. "Excuse me? Who are you?"

"I'm the guy who's been watching her while you were deployed, which I'm assuming is why she ended up on my porch." He blows out a breath, his voice taking on a softer tone. "Look, I'm sorry for bitching at you, but since I wasn't home last night, I'm a bit pissed we left her alone all night."

I sigh. My sleep schedule is all jacked up, so I know she's only been missing for maybe four hours at the most, and those were daylight hours. "I didn't fall asleep until well after four a.m. and she was with me when I did. Where are you? I'll come get her now."

"I'm at twenty-eight-seventeen K Street."

"Oh, thank god. You're only a few blocks from me. I'll be there in ten minutes."

"See you soon."

I hang up and run to the bathroom to brush my teeth and splash water on my face before piling my red hair on top of my head. Slipping on a pair of Vans, some ragged jean shorts, and a thin cotton T-shirt, I grab Sookie's leash and walk the four blocks to this stranger's house. I guess I should be thankful that if she was going to take off, it would be to someone who watched over her while I was gone.

I would like to thank him for the excellent care he provided, anyway. The weekly status reports I received from the center were god-sent and she always looked well cared for and happy.

Knocking on the glass storm door, I hear and then see two dogs—Sookie, followed by a dog who looks a lot like her, but is a tad smaller—rush into the living room. From behind them walks up the one man who has haunted my fantasies for the last six months.

"Oh, shit." I can't stop the words from flying out of my mouth.

He narrows his eyes, keeping the door between us shut. "You?"

"You're the trainer who took care of Sookie while I was gone?"

"Sookie's mom is the one who fucked me stupid and then snuck out before morning light?"

A deep blush hits my cheeks. "Uh…"

I glance at the front of the house and it all comes back to me. That night I was slightly intoxicated, but mostly I was so turned on I barely gave the house a second glance. It was only while he slept that I even had half a mind to clock where I was as I ordered an Uber back to the garrison. My surroundings from that night are a blur, but the man standing in front of me and the things he did to my body, as well as the things I did to his, are not.

"Oh shit," I say again.

He snorts and rolls his eyes, opening the door and inviting me in with a wave of his hand. "Come on in, *Cherise.*"

I can't help but notice how he enunciates every letter of my name, as if not knowing it has eaten at him since we met.

Sighing, I walk inside, immediately swarmed by two lovable fur balls. "Who is this?"

"That's Strijker. The two of them have grown very close over the last few months."

"He's beautiful." I pet him until I'm knocked on my ass by Sookie, who seems to be a bit of a jealous bitch when it comes to me. My dog sits in my lap while his dog rolls onto his back with his paws waving haphazardly in the air. I look up to find the man who rocked my world looming over us, staring down at me as if he's trying to reconcile the woman sitting in front of him with the woman he *fucked* so many months ago.

"So, you're John Vale, the veteran K9 trainer."

"I am." He offers me his hand. "At least now I know where you've been for the last six months. What I don't know is why you didn't tell me about your deployment that night and ghosted me before morning light?"

I bite my lip and look down at the dogs who are happy to wrestle gently over my legs. "Mari and I snuck out of garrison the night before shipping out. I didn't think I'd ever see you again, and I didn't want to start something hours before leaving for almost half a year. I mean, honestly, what were the odds we'd ever see each other again?"

"Considering I've been looking for you, I'd say the odds were pretty good." He sits down on an ottoman, leaning forward with his elbows on his splayed knees. Sitting in front of me, he confirms every memory I have of how sexy he is. It wasn't my imagination, nor my fantasies making him into more than I remember.

The man oozes sex appeal.

Absence might make the heart grow fonder, but does it make good memories out of blasé experiences?

I don't think so.

At least, I hope not.

"You've been looking for me?"

"Yeah." He rubs the back of his neck, his gaze bouncing around the room. "I had no intention of hitting and quitting it, although I suppose we never spoke about our intentions."

I smile and dip my head. I'm not feeling nearly as sexy or confident as I was the night I met him. In the morning light, after four hours of sleep with no makeup on, I doubt I'm rocking any sex appeal at all. "I don't remember a lot of words being exchanged between us that night."

"How about we start over?" He stands and offers me his hand. "My name is John Vale, but most people call me Vale. I'm new to town. Got here about six months ago after separating from the Army at Fort Liberty, North Carolina. What's your name?"

I take his hand and let him pull me to my feet. "Hi, Vale. My name is Cherise Jessica Taylor, but my friends call me Cher."

"Nice to meet you, Cher. Can I interest you in a cup of coffee? Maybe some breakfast?"

I glance down at the two fur balls who look very much at home and shrug, "If it's no trouble."

"No trouble at all."

Vale puts his hand on the small of my back and escorts me into the kitchen, where he leads me to a stool nestled against a granite island in the center of the room. "What do you take in your coffee?"

"Depends on how fancy you can get. I'll drink it black if I have to, but I prefer sweet and creamy."

He flashes me a sexy smile, letting me know he is fully aware of the double entendre, intended or otherwise.

That's the problem with working with men for six months straight. My mind is in the gutter. As a woman in a male-dominated field, I have to be aware of how a man's mind works, even if I have to feign obliviousness, just to make sure they don't think they have an opportunity with me. Mari and I have spent half a year making sure we don't cross any invisible lines drawn between the male and female soldiers in our unit.

It's just too messy otherwise.

"You bought furniture since the last time I was here."

I motion around the room, noting the dark and functional decor.

He places a cup of coffee on the counter in front of me and sets down a bottle of half-and-half and flavored creamer next to a spoon. "Yeah, I had been in this house for twelve hours when I met you, and I hadn't had time to go furniture shopping."

I nod, fixing my coffee with my eyes glued to the cup, my curiosity in overdrive. "It looks nice, but there are no real feminine touches to your decor."

He chuckles. "Is that your way of asking if I'm single?"

Biting my lip, I look up at him through my lashes as I stir my coffee. "Well, it has been six months."

"Six months since we last saw each other?" He leans across the island and rests his torso on his forearms, his face close enough to touch. His proximity sends his scent to my nostrils and I'm reminded of our night together when my body came alive in a way I've never before experienced—and probably never will again.

I stare at his sandy blonde hair, which is considerably lighter than when I met him last winter.

And lose myself in his green-gray eyes, committing every speck in his irises to memory.

My sexy man, John Vale, speaks to me on a cellular level, and I now know it wasn't just the thrill of that night that kept him visiting me day after day and night after night in vivid detail.

It wasn't the sneaking out.

Or breaking the rules.

Or alcohol.

Or the fantasy of being wild with no repercussions.

Right now, sitting inches from him, I feel energized despite my utter exhaustion.

It's not caffeine because I haven't sipped my coffee yet.

It's him.

"It's been six months since we last had anything with each other." I dare to bring up my gaze and meet his eyes, letting my unspoken sentiments be known with that simple sentence.

His lips twitch and his eyes turn molten. "It's been six months since I last had anything with anyone, period."

A light blush hits my cheek, but I'm not going to back down now. "It's been a long six months considering the memories you sent with me overseas. I've had a lot of time to replay every minute over and over again."

He sucks in his breath, his body rigid. "You should have told me who you were and where you were going. I could have sent you dirty notes and kept you primed until you got back."

I snort, breaking the spell between us. "Yeah, right? Women wait for their man to return from a deployment, but most men aren't signing up to wait on a woman—especially one they just met."

He pulls back and takes a thoughtful sip of his coffee, leaning his hip against the counter. "I used to deploy a lot, so I get it. But trust me, not all women wait."

"Bad breakup?"

"No worse than a lot of guys." He shrugs. "But that was a while ago."

I look away, questions that are too personal dancing on the tip of my tongue.

Too personal, Cher?

This man has been inside you.

He pulled your underwear off with his teeth.

He had you chanting out a deity's name as you came over and over again.

The absurd thought takes root in my brain, and I shake my head and giggle. "I can't believe I'm sitting in the kitchen of the only guy to ever give me multiple orgasms."

His coffee cup bounces off the granite and splashes over the top. "What?"

Oh my God, Cher! Did you really just say that out loud?

Slapping my hand over my mouth, I shake my head. "I'm so sorry. I didn't mean to say that with my outside voice."

VETERAN
K9
TEAM
REPORTING
FOR DUTY

Chapter 5
Vale

Every ounce of blood in my body leaves its assigned task and rushes straight to my cock. She's not the only one that's been playing that night on repeat, and while I remember her orgasming multiple times, I had no idea I was the only guy she's done it with.

That knowledge is going to mess with me for a while, inflating my ego back to a young man's proportions.

I meant to keep this casual.

I mean, I want us to get to know each other because the insane attraction between us and the spark that zings my awareness to life in her presence is very real. I recognized it the moment I saw her face through the glass storm door. Plus, the desire to sink between her creamy thighs is not going to abate soon.

Especially now.

Which means my dick isn't going to go soft soon.

Which means my brain is not going to function at one hundred percent—Any. Time. Soon.

I grab a couple of paper towels and quickly clean up my mess. "Was that a Freudian slip, or a carefully placed suggestion?"

Cher raises a brow and then shrugs her shoulder. "Honestly, I'm not sure."

I stare at her, taking in every freckle dotting her nose and cheeks. She wasn't wearing much makeup the night we met, but this morning she's scrubbed her face clean. Amazingly, she's even more beautiful than I remember and my hands itch to pull her hair out of the messy bun on top of her head and run my fingers through her long, silky strands.

"I've never felt drawn to someone like I am to you, Cher."

She smiles. "There is something here, isn't there? I felt you the moment you walked into the Last Stand that night. Like I was fully aware of you before I ever saw your face."

Taking a deep breath, I walk around the island and step between her splayed knees, her ass perched precariously on the wooden stool. I take liberty by sliding my hands over her hips and pressing my forehead to hers.

Just as I remember, she's beautiful and fearless, staring back at me with veiled anticipation.

"Have dinner with me tonight," I state versus ask.

She nods. "Okay."

"Do you like to camp? Hike? Fish?"

She licks her lips, her gaze bouncing from my eyes to my mouth. "Yes, to camping. Yes, to hiking. Not so much to fishing."

"I wanted to take the fur balls up into the national forest last spring, but I couldn't without your consent. Come with me and Strijker on Saturday and we'll make a day of it."

"That's four days from now." Cher wraps her fingers around my forearms, holding me in place. "Do you think we'll still be talking by then?"

"As long as you don't run away again—yes."

She grins. "You will never let me live that down, will you?"

I grin back, but my smile holds a hint of devilish joy. "I'll let you make it up to me... soon."

Pressing a chaste kiss against her lips, I close my eyes and savor the fantasy as it morphs into reality.

She's here.

My dream girl—the one I worried I had made up—is in my kitchen, drinking my coffee and about to eat my food.

I can't explain this soul-deep knowledge I have when it comes to her, but she admits to feeling it too. That's all the confirmation I need to pursue more.

Breaking our kiss, I take a step back. "How about some breakfast?"

"I'd love some."

"After we eat, if you're up for it, we can go to the park and I'll show you some of the recall commands I taught Sookie." I grab a carton of eggs out of the fridge and a pack of heat-and-eat sausages out of the freezer before snatching a pan out of the cabinet. "She's super smart and willing to obey—most of the time."

"She sounds like her momma." Cher hops off her stool and sits on the floor while I cook. Both dogs immediately swarm her, seeking cuddles and neck scratches. "How old is Strijker?"

"He's thirteen months—just a few weeks shy of Sookie."

"I don't remember you having a dog that night."

After throwing the sausage into the microwave, I crack six eggs into a bowl and whisk. "I didn't have a dog that night. Like I said, I'd barely moved into town a few days earlier and had closed on this house that morning."

"How does a K9 trainer not have his own dog?"

I dump the scrambled eggs into a pan and shrug. "Well, the dogs I trained were Army property, so you know where they are."

"In the Army," she says.

"Right. My last K9 is barely three years old and has another five years before she can retire. If her current trainer doesn't adopt her, I might." I stir the eggs until they are fluffy and then turn off the heat. "And my ex-wife took our dog with her when she left."

"You were married?"

I glance down at Cher on the floor with one hundred and ten pounds of fur draped over her lap. "I was. Nora didn't want a working dog, nor did she want a big dog to protect her while I was deployed. She wanted a lapdog, so we had a Papillon, which is a much smarter dog than you would think. I taught it how to do all kinds of stuff."

"Do you miss her?" Cher asks as she extricates herself from the floof and stands up.

"The dog?" I grin. "Sometimes."

She rolls her eyes and washes her hands in the sink. "I'm sorry I asked."

I press my chest against her back and slide my hands around her waist. Why the fuck do I feel so comfortable touching her in such an intimate way? Yes, we've fucked, but this is not that. This feels natural versus carnal.

It feels right.

She melts against my chest and tilts her head back to look up at me.

"You can ask me anything you want, Cher. I want to know you and I want you to know me. Nothing is off the table."

"Are you always so transparent with your one-night stands?" She goes for a smile, but it doesn't quite hit her eyes.

"I wish we hadn't started like that. I had full intentions of waking up and slipping back inside you, then taking a shower together before we went out for breakfast. Waking up alone was not part of my plan and, honestly, conducting myself that way isn't me. I've never been that kind of guy."

She glances down at the sink. "I don't go home with men I've just met, either. And I've never ducked out on one while he slept."

Inhaling deeply, I press a kiss to her temple and then lightly smack her ass. "Let's eat before the eggs get cold."

We take no time to scrape our plates clean. Cher is a woman who can eat and I think I might be in love. I hate it when women pick at their food like they're some fucking bird, afraid of enjoying what they put in their mouths. If I remember correctly—and I know I do—Cher is very enthusiastic about what she puts in her mouth.

"You want some more?" I take her plate, fully willing to cook a few more eggs and heat more sausage.

"No. If I eat too much, I'll pass out." She yawns and I'm remembering all the times I came back from the sandbox and slept for thirty-six hours straight. I don't think she's been home for over eighteen.

"You should be asleep right now," I say.

"Yeah, but Sookie won't let me." She smiles lovingly down at her dog.

"I tell you what. Let me throw on some shoes, and Strijker and I will escort you and Sookie home. If she's not ready for a nap by the time we get there, I'll bring her back here until our date tonight. That way, you can catch a few uninterrupted hours."

Cher laughs. "Is this your clever way of getting my address and ensuring I show up for our date tonight?"

"Yes." I don't even try to hide my ulterior motives.

"I like it." She stands and stretches her arms over her head, her thin cotton shirt riding up to show off a sliver of her soft belly. "We'll take an escort home."

Sookie does not settle down. If anything, I'd say she's even more amped up after introducing Strijker to her toys.

Cher kicks off her shoes and shimmies out of her shorts to reveal a pair of simple white cotton panties. They are the sexiest things I have ever seen, and I'm reminded of the pair of pink ones she left behind six months ago.

I should probably tell her I still have them buried in my nightstand, but admitting that might be too creepy.

Fuck. Now I'm wondering if I should throw them out.

Double fuck.

Cher slips between her smooth cotton sheets as I lean against the doorjamb, figuratively tucking her in for a long nap, while a coy smile plays at her lips. "Are you sure you don't want to take a nap with me?"

Every cell in my body awakens with the temptation and I do the hardest things I've had to do in a long time—I shake my head and take another step away from her. "Get some sleep. You'll need your energy to keep up with me tonight."

"Promise?"

"Definitely."

"Well then, good night John Vale, veteran K9 trainer."

I chuckle. "Sweet dreams, Cherise Jessica Turner."

"They will be now." She flashes me a wicked smile.

Growling low in my throat, I shake my head and turn

away, taking the dogs out of the house with me. I ensure the door locks behind me before Strijker, Sookie, and I jog back to my house to get the blood pumping through my veins and away from my cock where it has hung around for the last hour.

Jesus, this woman.

Twenty minutes later, we drive to the VKC for some afternoon playtime. I figure I'll want to tire out the kids as much as possible to make sure Cher and I have some semblance of a romantic evening. I haven't tested it to-date, but something tells me both of our fur babies are serious cock blockers.

Sookie is certainly a possessive one.

As soon as we walk through the door, Kemp eyes the dogs and then looks at me with a quizzical grimace furrowing his brow. "Aren't you supposed to be in the mountains?"

"I came home early."

He points to Sookie. "Did you steal the client's dog?"

"No." I take a deep breath, unable to wipe the shit-eating grin off my face. "Sookie belongs to *her*."

"*Her* who?"

"*Her*, man. The woman from the Last Stand. The woman from that night. She was deployed with her Army Reserve unit. Technically, she was AWOL when we met, and then she shipped out the next morning. That's why I haven't been able to find her."

Kemp runs his hand down his face and slumps into a chair. "Let me get this straight. Your one-night stand, the woman who fucked you stupid and then left you sideways without a name or a note—" he glances at the dogs "—is Sookie's mom?"

"Right?" I cross my arms and lean my shoulder blades against the wall near the door. "It's fucking fate."

"It's certainly something designed by a force beyond our comprehension." He shakes his head in disbelief.

"The gods brought her to me." I grin, feeling lighter than I have in years.

"Or the devil. Remember, Lucifer was once an angel, loved above all others." He frowns. "This is too weird."

I return his frown. "Man, don't ruin this for me. I'm happy."

Kemp shakes his head. "What do you know about her?"

"I know her name and where she lives." I push off the wall and toss my keys on the desk before grabbing a soda from our small tabletop fridge. "Tonight, I'll learn everything else I need to know."

He leans back in his chair and laces his fingers behind his head. I'm a big dude, but Kemp's biceps make me feel like a prepubescent boy who can't put on weight. The man lives in the gym to hide from his feelings. Some people eat—Kemp bench presses three hundred and fifty pounds without breaking a sweat. He's a beast. "Guard your heart, man. I'm not saying she can't be the one, but you fall harder than any guy I know, and I don't want to see you get hurt."

Again. The word goes unspoken, but I hear it just the same.

Anger simmers in my belly and my jaw clenches as I

search for the right words. I get he thinks he's protecting me, but all he's doing is pissing me off. Maybe I'm a bit of a romantic, but this isn't puppy love, nor is it desperation or loneliness.

This is deep-seated knowledge sent from on high.

How do I know? Why her?

I'm not going to fucking question what my heart knows to be true.

Be present in the moment.

Be willing to fail.

Be open to the universe to send you exactly what you need, when you need it.

Isn't that what the last year of self-help mumbo jumbo has told me?

Fuck what everyone else thinks. I'm running with this and straight to Cher if she'll have me.

"Man—" *Fuck you* is on the tip of my tongue, but I can't bring myself to say it. "I'm going to take the dogs out to the yard."

I walk out without a second glance in his direction, whistling for Sookie and Strijker to follow. Kemp's words buzz around my head, but they hold no heat as I run the dogs through a dozen drills. By the time we're done, the dogs are ready for water and a nap and I need a shower.

Kemp waits for me at his desk. The other trainer, Linc, stands with his back to us to block the doorway between the interview room and our office while talking to someone out of sight. Kemp leans forward to address me while stroking his glorious lumberjack beard. "I'm sorry I overstepped, Vale."

Sighing, I run my fingers through my sweat-soaked hair and grab a bottle of cold water out of our fridge while the pooches lap up water and crunch on the ice cubes Linc put in the bowl for his Husky, Li Lou. "You're just looking out for me. You're a damn good friend, Kemp."

He snorts. "Maybe I should start listening to some of those self-help books you listen to? You are way more emotionally mature than I am after all these years."

I chuckle. "Anytime you want to borrow one, let me know."

"Nanook! No!" a woman screams as a Husky between the size of Sookie and Strijker comes pushing past Linc into our office, his leash dragging behind him.

"Sitz," I say, causing Sookie and Strijker to take a seat, their gazes trained on Nanook as he runs right up to them without the caution I like to see strange dogs approach each other. Fortunately, Nanook's demeanor is friendly enough and they trust me with my one-word command for them to remain calm.

"Who is this?" I reach down and pet Nanook, who lowers himself into a playful crouch for the other dogs who have yet to move off their set point.

A short, curvy brunette pushes past Linc and snatches Nanook's leash off the ground. "I'm so sorry. Dammit, Nanook."

Linc chuckles from behind her. "This is our new client, Jamie, and her precocious Husky, Nanook."

She rolls her eyes and plasters on a patient smile. "Nanook is supposed to be an emotional support animal, but I'm struggling with him during our VA center visits."

"The VA center?" I glance at Linc and then Kemp. It's always good to meet another military or ex-military support person in the area.

Nodding, she bends down and gives loving pets to Sookie and Strijker. "Yeah, I'm a PTSD counselor contracted to the VA regional center, as well as the county's first responder support unit. Most of my interaction is telework, but I want to train Nanook to serve as an emotional support animal so I can do in-person visits to the center. Unfortunately, on our last visit, Nanook ate a cheeseburger out of one of the veteran's hands while we weren't paying attention, and they promptly kicked us out of the dining area."

She shakes her head and looks up at me. "It was so embarrassing."

I grin, pressing my lips together to suppress my chuckle while Linc boldly laughs behind her.

Chuckling herself, she waves her hand. "Go ahead and laugh, guys. My fiancé did when I told him."

"Well, it looks like we have the temperament test complete. He's a super friendly dog."

"Too friendly with absolutely no shits to give in following directions." She sighs.

Linc tilts his head to me. "I figured we could tag team his training."

I nod. "Yeah. Schedule it up and let me know."

"Oh, thank god," she breathes, taking a step back from us. "Look how well-behaved your dogs are. That's amazing! Can you train him to do that?"

"Definitely." I bend down and rub Nanook's head. "How old is he?"

"Twelve months." She bites her lip, as if she knows she's a good six months behind on his training.

"Close to these two in age. He'll learn a lot from them."

"And us," Linc scoffs.

"Yeah and us." I grin, releasing her dog to stand. I can tell Nanook is going to be a good student as he reads and mimics Sookie and Strijker's contained excitement. They are dying to be released from the set points and show their eagerness by glancing up at me often, whining softly as huskies are apt to do. Unfortunately, we don't have the room in the office for three near full-sized huskies to play.

"Well, it was nice to meet everyone. Again, sorry he barged in like that." Jamie tightens up on his leash, letting him know to pay attention to her. They turn around and walk past Linc, back into the interview room.

"Bye Nanook." Kemp chuckles.

This time, Linc closes the door behind him, and I release the dogs from their set point. They are instantly up with their noses to the ground, sniffing and memorizing the new dog's scent.

"Guess you'll have to convince Sookie's mom to bring her in for training and doggie playdates."

"It should be easy if we're spending our nights together," I proclaim boldly.

Kemp presses his lips together and nods, his eyes going to the paperwork on his desk. I shake my head, letting his negativity and unsaid comments remain unspoken. No reason to fight with him when he's already in my head.

"I'm going to head out and take the two fur balls home. See you tomorrow," I say, clipping their leashes on their collars and walking toward the door.

"Yeah, man. I'll see you tomorrow," Kemp says to my retreating back.

VETERAN
K9
TEAM
REPORTING
FOR DUTY

Chapter 6
Cher

I wake up from a four-hour nap disoriented.

Again.

This wasn't my first deployment, but it was only my second—so, not exactly a pro, but not an amateur either. There is a thirteen-and-a-half-hour difference between Afghanistan and Colorado, the perfect separation between day and night to screw up your sleep schedule.

As soon as I remember where I am, I stretch out and flex my muscles, an ache between my legs building with no prompting. Green-gray eyes and sandy blonde hair fill me with warmth as I imagine the square jawline and sexy smirk on Vale's lips.

I can't believe the guy I've been pining over for six months has been training and caring for Sookie. And she loves him—that much is obvious. After twelve hours with me, once I wasn't paying attention to her, she sought him and Strijker out.

What am I going to do about that?

I knew leaving her was going to be hard, but coming home and getting her to accept me again is even harder.

How do I deal with her bonding with another person? Especially a person I, too, have pseudo-bonded to. I mean, I had no intention of finding him, but I'd be lying if I didn't admit to already having plans to hang out at the Last Stand with Mari next weekend—you know, just in case.

But now I don't have to worry about it taking weeks or months to run into him.

Sookie brought him right to me. If that isn't cosmic forces, I don't know what is.

The ache between my legs is ever-present, and this is what happens when a woman doesn't masturbate for six months. Time alone is rare. You share a room with at least one, but sometimes up to three other women. If you're lucky, you split shifts with your roommates, which gives you a bit of alone time, but that didn't happen for me this time.

Besides, it's not like I deployed with a vibrator in my duffle bag.

Memories of having Vale between my thighs have me scissoring my legs in my sheets.

I'll see him tonight. The attraction between us is off the charts. But he seems to hold himself back too.

I mean, if he'd made the slightest move toward his bedroom this morning, I would have gone.

Then I invited him to tuck me into my bed, but he said no.

Can't blame a girl for trying.

I was truthful when I said that I'd never gone home with a guy after a couple of rounds of pool, but there is something about Vale that makes my knees fall open.

I grab my phone to check the time and find a couple of missed text messages.

Vale: Good evening, sweetness. I hope you slept well. The dogs have been exercised and fed, so they should be good while we're out. Can I pick you up at six?

Six sounds amazing.

Vale arrives at my house with Sookie and Strijker in tow.

"I thought you'd leave them at your place?" I was thinking if they were at his house, he could smoothly invite me over—not that he'd have to coax me back into his bed.

He swings open my door, and the dogs bound in ahead of him. Strijker immediately sniffs every corner and every piece of furniture like he wasn't here six hours ago. "They'll be fine here. Besides, since I'm driving, I have to swing by here to drop you off, anyway. Are you okay with having Strijker in your house while we're gone?"

"Sure. Does he need to be crated or something?" I

watch as Sookie bounds over to her toy box, just like she did when I brought her home yesterday, immediately pulling the tattered remains of plushies and rope bones for Strijker's inspection.

But it's Vale's use of the words *drop you off* that sticks with me. Does he not plan to spend the night with me?

Vale shakes his head. "I leave them loose in the house and so far, we've only had one incident involving a teddy bear I won at a fair. The dogs shredded it like cotton candy."

"Yeah, Sookie performs squeakectomies on most of her plushies." I turn to grab my wallet and catch him checking me out, heat sizzling behind his gaze.

"You look beautiful," he says, his eyes and voice saying *do me, do me NOW*, but his hands are clenched at his sides and he doesn't make a move toward me.

"Are you okay?"

He nods, flexing his fingers and then offering me his hand. "I'm good. How about you?"

"I'm fine." I interlace my fingers with his, the electricity of his touch traveling up my arm.

I think he feels it too, because he looks at our joined hands, brings them up to his mouth and kisses my fingertips. "I didn't make a reservation anywhere because I thought after six months of chow hall and ready-to-eat meals, you might have a few favorites you missed."

"Mmmm." The man knows what it's like to come home after a deployment. "How do you feel about Italian?"

"Love it."

"There is an amazing neighborhood hole-in-the-wall on the west side called Mama Napoli's."

He holds open the door, ushering me outside. "Let's go."

We drive the ten miles from my house to the restaurant. Vale is a perfect gentleman—meaning he opens doors and escorts me by placing his hand on my back. I'm a tall girl, so things like that really register with me. Many men assume because I'm a big girl, I can handle it myself.

Or I insist on handling it myself.

While I could do it myself, this time I don't want to. I enjoy feeling watched over and protected—trusted to take care of myself and yet made to feel like I don't have to.

It makes me feel cherished.

There is nothing sexier.

When we are seated, the server smiles down at me. "Hey, sugar. Where have you been?"

"I was out of the country."

"Ah. Well, I'm glad you're back. Who's this handsome man?"

"This is Vale, and it's his first time." I grin, waggling my brows at him. "Do you trust me to order for us?"

He raises his brow and sets aside his menu. "Absolutely."

"Any allergies or extreme dislikes before I order?"

"I'll eat anything you put in front of me." His voice lowers an octave, making my insides clench in anticipation. Who would have thought after one night together my pussy would have muscle memory? But it does, and just the sound of his voice causes her to pulse with need.

"Oh," the server whispers at the same time I say, "I remember that about you."

Vale flashes an evil grin and then directs his eyes to our server, who is glancing between us and fanning herself.

"We'll have a half-order of manicotti, baked lasagna, Caesar salad, garlic focaccia bread with extra garlic and an order of calamari to start," I say.

She nods. "And to drink?"

I look at Vale. "Are you a wine drinker?"

He nods.

"We'll take a bottle of red," I say, smiling as she walks away.

"Red?" Vale says with a chuckle.

"They're small and their menu is solid, but their wine selection is literally red or white. Not bad, not amazing, but pairs well enough with their food."

Vale shrugs and clasps his hands on the table. "I'm not a connoisseur, so I'm sure it will be fine."

"It takes a confident man to let a woman order for him." I slide my palm over his hands, using the tip of my index finger to draw small circles on his wrist.

His gaze fixes on the small action, and when he brings his eyes up to mine, they are ablaze with something. Heat? Desire? Emotion? Anger?

It's not as easy to tell as it was this morning.

"Confident, huh?"

"I think so." I pull my hand back when the server comes back with two glasses and a bottle of wine. Thankfully, she hands the bottle to him and asks if he wants to pour. He does and then I'm holding up my glass. "Should we toast?"

"Welcome home," he says with a tilt of his head.

"Here is to the cosmic coincidences that brought us together again."

Taking a deep breath, he closes his eyes, nods and then takes a sip.

"Are you okay?" I know I've already asked him this once, but he is not the guy I met this morning. He's battling something in his head, but I don't know what. I was asleep all afternoon, so I can't imagine what I did to fuck up already.

"Do you believe in fate?" he asks as he sets his wine glass down.

I lean back, my grip tightening on my stem. "I believe we make decisions that guide our path, but I also believe there are certain lessons your soul is supposed to learn on each incarnation and those are unavoidable. How the lesson gets taught to your soul comes from the decisions you make along the way. Why?"

"When I took the dogs to the center today, my buddy told me to slow my roll and guard my heart."

I arch my brow. "Oh?"

"He was there for me when I went through my separation, and he thinks he's looking out for me."

I sigh and take a deep drink from my wine glass. "So, you're saying you don't want to get married this weekend?"

Chuckling, he brings his eyes down to the table. "I know I sound stupid."

"Your ex really did a number on you, huh?"

He exhales a big breath and rolls his shoulders back. "Honestly, no. I mean, I was blindsided, so I've spent a lot of time working on myself, trying to make myself a better, less selfish person. But Kemp thinks I fall too easily."

"Oh." I press my lips together and say nothing as the server puts down a plate of calamari and walks away. "And what do you think, Vale?"

"I think if I fell easily, I'd be shacked up with someone I had lukewarm feelings for. But I'm not. And with you, I just know. I knew it the moment I saw you."

I bite my lip and swallow down the *squee* threatening to erupt from my lips. I get his friend's concern—I really do. And if I'd been truly heartbroken before, maybe I would be a bit more cautious. I've had teenage heartbreak, but I've never felt half of what I felt after one night with my mystery man, John Vale.

And I believe in living every day to the fullest, without fear, without reservation.

Why else would I be in the Army?

I squeeze a slice of lemon over the calamari. "Would it make you feel better to know I've spent the last six months kicking myself in the ass for not exchanging my information with you? And Mari and I already had plans to go to the Last Stand this Saturday to hang out."

He grins. "Was that your stomping grounds before you left?"

I giggle. "No. I'd gone there a handful of times over the last couple of years, but I'm not a regular."

Reaching across the table, he asks for my hand. "Were you going there to find me?"

I slide my fingers into his warm palm, but because I'm a brat and I can't stroke his ego too hard or give up the compliments that easily, I narrow my eyes and shake my head. "I was going there to hang out with my friend, but if I ran into you again..."

Chuckling, he squeezes my hand and stabs a forkful of calamari with his other. He offers me the first bite. "That does make me feel better."

"Good. So, let's just roll with this. Have fun and see what happens."

"I like that."

VETERAN
K9
TEAM
REPORTING
FOR DUTY

Chapter 7
Vale

I could kill Kemp for getting into my head. Now I feel like an asshole for letting him affect my mood—for making me build walls around my heart.

No risk, no reward.

"What do you say to a couple of rounds of pool after this? We could make a wager." I waggle my brow.

"That sounds like a perfect way to start over," she says with a smile.

"I think so, too."

The server comes with our salad, and a few minutes later, our entrees. We eat it all, and it's the best Italian food I've had outside of Italy itself.

"You were right. This was amazing. I can't believe we ate it all."

"I'm a big girl. I need my food." She pats her belly.

"You're perfect, and I think it's unbelievably sexy that you enjoy good food. I didn't think we'd eat it all when you ordered it."

"Well, we did. Extra garlic and all."

I motion to the server and hand her my credit card before Cher can open her mouth. "Don't think extra garlic will stop me from kissing you later."

"How much later?" She raises her brow.

I change chairs and sit next to her, interlacing my fingers with hers and resting her hand on my thigh. "Are you waiting for me to kiss you?"

"No," she says, leaning forward and pressing her lips onto mine. I slide my fingers into her silky hair, fisting a handful as I take over, tilting her head so I can deepen the kiss. Her lips are just as I remember, sweet and sassy, demanding and pliable. She's the kind of woman who gives as good as she gets, and I'm here for every ounce of it.

I pull back and look into her bright green eyes. "If I keep kissing you, I'm not going to be able to stand up from this table without offending the other patrons."

She giggles. "Maybe we should go back to my place?"

"What about playing pool?"

"We can do that another night."

Pressing my forehead to hers, I sigh. I want to. God, do I want to. I am only a man, for fuck's sake. But if we build a relationship on sex, what else will there be? "If we burn too hot—"

"What?" she interrupts me. "We'll fizzle out? I don't think so, Vale. You can wine and dine me, but you can also fuck me. We are past the point of pretenses, don't you think?"

"I suppose we are, but we're staying at your place tonight." I lightly tug her hair and flash her a smile.

"So I can't sneak out?"

"Exactly."

wo unapologetic fur balls meet us at the door, white puffs of cotton strewn across the living room floor.

"Shit," I mutter, disappointed in the kids.

"They'll be fine, huh?" she says with a wry smile on her face as she kicks off her shoes.

"What did they tear up?" I search the floor, kneeling to untie my boots.

She picks up the remains of Sookie's dog bed. "Found it."

"Shit," I say again. "I'm sorry."

Cher laughs, picking up tufts of cotton from the floor. "Maybe we should have stayed in tonight?"

"They know better than to tear shit up. We've been working on it for months, but they're acting out for your attention."

She puts two giant handfuls of cotton in the trash and then plops down on the floor to be consumed by floof. "It's working because they now have my attention."

I love how she is with the dogs. She's not mad, or if she is, she isn't yelling at them. It would be fruitless to scold the dogs after the deed is done, anyway. And so, she cleans up the mess and gives them what they want. Attention.

I sit on the ground behind her, straddling her between my thighs. Cher leans back and puts her head on my shoulder and we're as comfortable as an old couple who have known each other forever.

"Hi." She smiles up at me.

I dip my face and press my lips where her neck meets her shoulder. "Hi back."

Using my left hand, I scratch Strijker behind the ears while I wrap my other around Cher's waist, cupping her breast and pulling her against me. "I like how you are with the dogs."

"How's that?"

"Patient. These breeds need a lot of training and understanding."

She has Sookie between her legs, rolling back and forth from her left to her right—her paws batting at the air. Cher has one hand dug into her fur, the other on my thigh, inching toward my groin.

The higher she moves her hand, the less attention Strijker gets and soon I have both my hands on her, pulling her T-shirt up to knead her breasts. I suckle her neck and trail kisses to her ear, sucking her lobe in between my lips.

She arches her back, pushing her ass into my cock, her fingers digging into my thigh.

Fucking sweet god, this woman is perfect for me.

I growl and slide a hand between her legs. A deep

need to strip her and explore every inch of her body takes over, and I think the dogs can fend for themselves for a couple more hours.

If they eat her couch, I'll buy her a new one.

"I need to get you naked."

She grins. "It's about time, Vale."

Scrambling to my feet, I grab her hand and pull her up. Then I wrap my arms around her, pinning her to my chest, cupping her head and kissing her with six months' worth of pent-up need and aggression. My heart says never let her go, but my mind is currently fucking with me. I meant every word I said to her, but I now have this nagging fear telling me to guard my heart.

Stupid fucking Kemp. I'm going to make him pay —somehow.

But I will do everything I can to give her nothing less than all of me tonight, because anything less would cheat us both. And hopefully, after spending a night between her thighs, I'll wake up with my head out of my ass.

Cher melts in my arms, mewling and rubbing her body against mine. I slide my hands under her ass, lifting her off her feet.

She yelps and wraps her legs around my waist. "Vale!"

"Yeah, baby?" I carry her back toward her bedroom, the one it took everything within me to leave her lying in hours ago.

"I can't believe you're carrying me."

"You're not as big as you think you are. As a matter of fact, you fit perfectly in my hands." Kissing her neck, I toe the door open and then kick it shut, locking the two fur balls out. I sit down with Cher in my lap, kissing her until we are both breathless. Just like the night we met, she isn't shy in the slightest, pulling off her shirt and flinging it across the room. Then she grasps at my shirt, insisting I raise my arms so she can pull the fabric free. As soon as my shirt is off, my hands are on her, flicking open the clasp of her bra and sliding the cups off her breasts.

I'd say I was an ass man, but something about Cher's breasts has haunted my dreams. She is lush—more than a handful—and drool-worthy and I can imagine waking up every morning fondling and teasing her awake.

I bury my face in her cleavage, rolling her nipples between my thumbs and forefingers.

She moans and tosses her head back to let me know how much she likes it.

Just as I remember, so fucking responsive.

I roll her onto her back while her fingers grapple with my belt.

"I want you inside of me."

Chuckling, I unfasten her jeans and lift off of her. "And I want to be inside of you, but first, I need to taste every inch of you."

She lifts her hips so I can pull her jeans off her long legs, leaving her bare to my gaze. Christ, she's even more beautiful than I remember. That night was a blur, but at the time I didn't know I needed to memorize it.

I won't make that mistake again.

"I love your long legs. Thick and muscular and perfect to wrap around my head."

"You say the sweetest things." She moans as I muscle my way between her thighs and bury my face into her pussy, licking and sucking before she can ask me to stop.

Not that I think she would ask me to stop.

She fists a handful of my hair and jerks her pussy against my mouth, riding my face with the same no-nonsense need as she took her pleasure from me last time. I fucking love that about her.

"Oh, yes!" she moans. "Yes, Vale."

I like hearing my name on her lips. John or Vale or both—it doesn't matter, as long as she is here with me.

"Are you going to come for me, Cher?"

"Yes." She groans at the same time her thighs squeeze my head.

She crumbles, her climax turning her into a convulsing, quivering mess. Coming hard, she floods my mouth with her sweet cream. I drink down every drop, reveling in her taste, her smell—everything. I don't want to forget a thing, just in case.

She's gasping for breath when her legs fall open and I crawl up her body, a satisfied smirk on my lips. "I love how you come."

"I love how you make me come." Her voice is husky, dripping with desire. "Now, I want to make you feel good, too."

She rolls me onto my back, working the fly of my jeans open and yanking them down my hips. I'm hard and aching and my cock springs free with a not-so-gentle tug of my pants. "Mmmm." She licks her lips and smiles down at me. "I've been dreaming about this."

"You've been dreaming about sucking my cock?" I raise my brow and groan as she rubs her thumb through the pre-cum dripping from the head.

"I've been dreaming about making you moan my name." She gives me a saucy wink before lowering her head. Her slick tongue licks me from base to tip before she wraps her lips around my length and takes me deep in her hot, wet mouth. My eyes flutter closed, and I let my head drop back, groaning my pleasure. "Oh, fuck me, Cher. You feel amazing."

She works me perfectly with her hand and her mouth, sucking and stroking me with complete confidence. Within minutes, my balls tighten up and I'm on the verge of coming.

"Stop. Stop stop stop." I cup her cheek and slide my fingers into her hair, pulling her off me. "I don't want to come yet."

"Do you have condoms?" She slides to the floor, taking my pants off the rest of the way.

"In my wallet."

"Good. Because the ones I have in my drawer are a couple of years old and I'm not sure if they're good anymore." She tosses me my billfold and then crawls onto the bed next to me, tracing her fingertips through the hair on my chest.

I pull out the three I have with me and set them on the nightstand. "If we need more than three, we'll have to check out those expiration dates."

"I can't wait." She grins.

Shaking my head at my little tease, I sheath my

aching cock and roll her to her back, settling myself between her legs. "I've been fantasizing about doing this again for months."

"Feels like a lifetime." Cher cups my face and kisses me with a possession I feel down in my toes.

For the first time in six months, I spread her wide and slide into her heat—finally, feeling like I'm home.

VETERAN
K9
TEAM
REPORTING
FOR DUTY

Chapter 8
Cher

I gasp, the feel of Vale stretching and filling me takes my breath away.

God, I feared I'd made up how good he feels, but he's even better than I remembered. The curve of his cock hits me just right, stroking and caressing my g-spot—and he has a way of knowing exactly how slow or fast I need him to go. He pulls up my thigh, bracing it with his forearm, sliding in and out at the perfect angle and hitting me just right.

"Fuck, I thought your mouth was heaven, but your cunt would make the angels sing," he growls in my ear, nibbling my neck.

I chuckle, scraping my fingers against his scalp. "Your cock is pretty magical, too."

Vale continues to work himself in and out of me, causing me to gush until I'm soaking wet, arousal dripping out of me. "I want you to come for me again and again. Your body is mine, Cher. Your orgasm—mine."

"And my heart?" I pant as my climax builds, my inner walls clamping down around his thick length.

"Mine!" he grunts, his thrusts coming quicker and harder.

I splinter apart, a small orgasm releasing seconds before a harder one hits, causing my body to shake and my heart to swell.

He roars as he pumps his hips faster, chasing his release, his cock jerking and throbbing inside of me. "Fuck, I love being inside of you."

"I love you, too."

Time stops and then Vale collapses on top of me, his body tight, muscles bunched underneath my hands. We're panting as we fight to catch our breath and I realize what I've said—answering a declaration he never made.

Shit! I knew I was feeling a certain way, but did I mean it?

Do I love John Vale?

I panic, wondering if he'll save me my embarrassment by ignoring my bold proclamation.

Or will he answer me? Does he love me too? I know he's afraid of falling for me, but has he already fallen, or is he in the process of walling off his heart?

After thirty seconds, he pulls out and rolls to my side, pulling me into his arms but not looking me in the eye. "Wow. That was even better than I remembered," he says and my heart breaks a bit.

He's going to ignore it—for now.

For forever, maybe.

"I'm going to clean up." Vale swings his legs off the

bed and walks into the bathroom, pulling off the condom as he walks away. I watch his broad back and tight ass as he strides from the bed and closes the door behind him. Lying back against the pillow, I stare up at the ceiling.

Do I love him?

Yes, I think I do. I've never felt about someone the way I feel about him. Tuned in from the moment our eyes met, I've been dreaming about him all this time. I was worried that absence makes the heart grow fonder, and that I was making him into something more than he was, but he's been perfect since the moment he eyeballed me through his glass security door.

The toilet flushes, the sink turns on and two minutes later, Vale is sliding beside me on the bed, pulling me back into his chest. He nibbles on my neck. "I'm going to fuck you all night, but I do have to work in the morning."

"You do?"

"Yeah. But I promise to wake and kiss you before I leave."

I snort. "You're not going to sneak out?"

"What good would that do?" he chuckles. "You know where I live."

Glancing over my shoulder, I reach back and cup him, finding him hard and ready for me again. "That's right, I do. There's no running away from me, John Vale, and don't you forget it."

We make love all night long, using all three of his condoms and two of mine.

Who knew the expiration dates on those were good for so many years?

I'll get the ring or an IUD if we continue to see each other because I want nothing between us for any longer than necessary. Neither of us has been with anyone else since we met six months ago, but before that? I know I'm STI-free because I got checked as part of my physical before we deployed, but I don't know what Vale was doing before he moved to Spring City.

Maybe he went wild after his divorce?

I mean, I fell into bed with him after two hours of playing pool—so the idea isn't out of bounds. Nauseating —because I can't stand the idea of anyone else touching him—but it's not out of the realm of possibilities.

I text him around lunch to ask what he is doing after work.

He doesn't reply.

Around six, I send him another text.

Hey, you. Long day?

We both have iPhones and I see he has read my messages. I prefer to not come across as a crazy person, so I wait a few minutes, giving him a chance to respond.

Maybe he's driving.

Maybe he's in the middle of a conversation and can't type out a response.

Sookie and I head out for a walk and I'm hoping we can stop by his house and say hello, but if he doesn't respond to my texts, I can't drop by without coming off as some stalker psycho chick, now can I?

When fifteen minutes pass without a response, I get pissed.

> Are you ghosting me?

Bubbles. Three dots letting me know he's receiving, reading, and responding.

> No, I'm not ghosting you.

> Okay. Are you still at work?

> No, I got off at four, but Strijker and I are hiking in the mountains.

> The mountains? I didn't realize you had plans. Sorry for bothering you.

> You're not bothering me. I'm on a local trail trying to clear my head.

> Clear your head?

Three bubbles...

> I need some time to think.

Staring at my phone, I shake my head. Anger, confusion and heartbreak battle to take over my mind. Gritting my teeth, I typed out another message.

> Take all the time you need, Vale. I won't bother you.

Ten seconds later, my phone rings and I answer it. "Yeah?"

"Don't be mad."

"I'm not mad. Take whatever time you need. Call me when you figure it out."

"I don't want to lose you, Cher." His voice sounds choked, the words strangled.

I glance down at Sookie, who sits beside me patiently. "Then what do you want?"

"I... I'm working on it."

Sighing, a rogue tear falls down my cheek. "I'm not going to sit here and wait for you to figure it out. Mari asked me to go out tonight, so I'll be out with her."

"Where will you be?"

"I don't think you're in a position to ask me that right now. Do you?"

Vale meets me with a moment of silence. "No, I suppose I'm not."

VETERAN
K9
TEAM
REPORTING
FOR DUTY

Chapter 9
Vale

M y next phone call is to Kemp, but I get that out-of-range / no cell service recording from my wireless carrier.

Weird. I just called and messaged Cher with no problem.

Then I notice I have no signal. No bars at all.

"Come on, Strijker. Let's head home."

Strijker bounds down the trail ahead of me at a much faster pace than he ascended the mountain, as if he knows where we are going and, more importantly, to whom.

Down at my truck, in the parking lot at the base of the trailhead, I have a signal.

"Hey," Kemp answers my call wearily. To be fair, I did snap at him all day. I was a grumpy SOB for a guy who'd had sex all night.

Cher said she loved me, but she said it as a response to words that never came out of my mouth. Oh, don't get me wrong, they wanted to, but somehow I kept that shit locked down. Between being afraid of saying those three blasted words and feeling like a jackass for not acknowledging them once she said them, I was in a horrible mood today despite the best sex of my life.

I'm a fucking idiot.

"Grab Linc and meet me at my house."

"Why?"

"We're going out. You're going to be my wingmen and hopefully entertain a cute little chick named Mari while I'm proclaiming my love for Cher."

Kemp sighs. "Man, I can't tell if you had an amazing or horrible night last night. You were a dick today."

"I know, and I'm sorry, but this is partly your fault."

"I figured," he grumbles.

"Call Linc, get dressed, slap on some cologne or whatever fruity shit you wear, and be at my house in forty-five minutes."

He sighs. "Alright, see you in forty-five."

We walk into the Last Stand and it's like I'm reliving a scene from six months ago. Cher and Mari are at the pool table, cues in hand. Her eyes meet mine as soon as I step across the threshold, as if she felt me as soon as I pulled into the parking lot. I knock Kemp on the arm and motion to the table, walking up with a roll of quarters already cupped in my hand.

"Can I play the winner?"

Cher has the eight ball lined up and looks up at me through her lashes. "That would be me."

"I hoped that would be the case."

I turn to her short, curvy friend and offer my hand. "Mari, I assume?"

She smiles up at me. She's a pretty girl. Easy on the eyes with a smirk planted on her full lips. One look at her and I know she's a troublemaker.

"Three hotties. Y'all are giving my reverse harem fantasies a starring lineup. Too bad at least one of you isn't available."

I chuckle and then gesture to the guys with me. "These are my buddies, Kemp and Linc. Kemp's buying the next round. Can you help him order the right drinks?"

He sighs, shakes his head and then plasters on a smile as he offers her his arm. "This way, mi'lady."

Mari hands me her pool stick and lowers her voice. "You have some major ass-kissing to do, buddy."

Nodding, I bring my eyes up to Cher. "I know. Take your time coming back with those drinks."

I grab the triangle, push my quarters into the coin slide, and rack the balls. "How about we make this interesting?"

Cher stares at me, no smile lighting up her beautiful face, and chalks the tip of her queue. "What did you have in mind?"

"Just a little wager." I remove the triangle and walk over to her end of the table, taking the discarded chalk off the bumper.

"I'm listening."

I set the chalk down and lean forward, inhaling her floral scent. "If you lose, you have to come home with me tonight."

She quirks an eyebrow. "Really? That's a bold bet, considering the last time all you wanted was a simple kiss."

"I think we're beyond simple kisses now, don't you?"

"Touché. And if I win?"

I grin and put my mouth near her ear. "What do you want?"

She lays her hand over my left pec. "I want your heart."

"You've already got it, Cher."

"Are you sure about that?" She turns her face, her lips less than an inch from mine.

"Yes. I went for a hike to look for a sign that we weren't moving too fast and that my feelings were real. Then my phone beeps with an incoming message in an area where I shouldn't have had cell service. And then— with no bars, no signal—I called and heard your voice crystal clear." I cup her cheek and rub my thumb over her bottom lip. "Or more to the point, I heard the pain in your voice and knew I was fucking up and needed to come home right away—to find you and let you know I love you and I don't fucking care if it's too soon to say it."

I capture her lips, and she melts into me.

Thank God.

"I love you, Cher."

"I love you, too, Vale."

Kissing her again, I slide my tongue into her mouth and lean my body against hers, claiming her for everyone to see. I only stop when I hear Mari giggling and Kemp clearing his throat. "Dude."

Growling, I lean my forehead against Cher's and smile. "So, about that wager. Are you willing to lose to me?"

Cher smiles back at me. "Even if I lose, it sounds like I've already won."

VETERAN
K9
TEAM
REPORTING
FOR DUTY

Epilogue
Cher - Three and a half years later

Arrrraaaauuuoooowwww.

Sookie bitches at me as a litter of puppies stumble over themselves to grab her attention. They mewl and whine with their displeasure as she fights to get away from them. They're at that age where they still nuzzle momma for milk and yet are too big to depend on her alone. I just fed them puppy mush. Some of their faces are still covered in gruel.

Cari, our oldest daughter, reaches up for a wet paper towel. "I do it."

"Be gentle." I remind her, handing her one towel so that she can wipe the puppies' faces.

She's just shy of three years old. Our son is twenty months.

That's right—do the math.

I never had time to get an IUD or a birth control ring. Vale and I got pregnant during my three weeks off before reporting back for duty—probably that first night.

Condoms might have expiration dates years in the future, but it has been my experience that their effectiveness dwindles with every passing day.

More math—I've been pregnant damn near nonstop since we got together.

Children hadn't even been a thought before seeing that first pink plus sign, but the moment I saw it, I knew it was not only going to be okay, but that this was exactly what was supposed to happen for us.

Vale asked me to marry him that weekend and by the end of the month, we were man and wife. Three months later, Sookie went into heat and two months after that she had her first litter—Christmas puppies—with Strijker, who turned out to be the perfect mate.

"All clean, Mommy." Cari runs to the kitchen garbage and throws her trash away.

"Shhh. Johnnie's asleep." I rub my belly, suspecting all the rumors about the third child are about to come true. First trimester, I could barely leave the bed without a puke pail attached to my neck. Second trimester, I was exhausted and having muscle cramps in places I didn't even realize were muscles. I thought I was ready to pop at the end of the seventh month... which means the last five weeks have been utter hell.

Add in Sookie getting accidentally pregnant—me way too sick to pay attention to her heat schedule—and it's been a rough holiday season.

"Hey, baby." Vale walks in with two bags of groceries and a bouquet of assorted flowers.

"Daddy!" Cari rushes him, her excitement causing

the puppies to yip and yowl, but thankfully doesn't wake our son from his nap.

Vale stoops down and lifts our daughter with one arm, leaning forward and kissing my cheek. "Go sit down and I'll bring you a snack."

"Okay," I sigh, easing myself down into the recliner. In the living room is an undecorated tree, boxes of ornaments strewn across the floor and tinsel everywhere.

They come back ten minutes later, Cari with a small plastic bowl of her own. Vale hands me a plate of cut-up fruit—some of the only food I can stomach right now—and kneels beside me, taking my foot in his hands. He slides his thumb up the arch of my foot, causing me to moan.

"You okay, Mommy?" Cari says over a mouth of mac-n-cheese. "That's your daddy night night noise."

Truthfully, Mommy hasn't let Daddy make her make the night night noise in weeks.

Everything is sensitive.

Too damn sensitive.

Vale chuckles and shakes his head. "She's too smart sometimes."

"Maybe we should soundproof our bedroom." I grimace, a Braxton-Hicks contraction causing me to grit my teeth.

He moves up my legs, rubbing small circles over my round, tight belly. "Real one?"

"I don't think so."

"Why don't you take a nap? We'll wake you up after we have the tree decorated."

"Come here." I crook my finger, smiling as he comes up and nuzzles my neck.

"Yes, baby?"

I kiss his cheek and run my fingers through his thick hair. "I love you, but after I have this kid, you are getting the snippy snip."

He chuckles. "I already have an appointment."

"You do?" I sigh, rubbing my belly again.

"Late January. Sookie and Strijker both have their appointments in early January after we re-home all the puppies. By Valentine's Day, the Vale baby factories will be closed."

"Thank you, honey. While I love making babies with you, the last two times haven't been nearly as much fun as the first time."

"For you and Sookie both. I see the way you both look at me—like you want to take a bite out of my ass."

"Mmmm. I can't wait to do that again, you know?"

Vale kisses me—sweetly, then possessively—growling under his breath. "Me neither."

VETERAN
K9
TEAM
REPORTING
FOR DUTY

Second Epilogue
Vale - Two years later

"Are you sure about this?" Cher looks Mari in the eye as she hands over Jessie's diaper bag.

"We'll be fine." Mari rolls her eyes and shakes her head in my direction.

"Where's the brute?" I ask, expecting Kemp to be here.

"He ran to the store. He should be back any minute." She shrugs and set the diaper bag down next to the two overnight bags we packed for the kids. Our eldest, Cari, is five and in kindergarten, and an expert on everything. Just ask her. Johnnie is a little over three and a half, and was hell-on-wheels until Jessie came into the world. The baby of the Vale family came into the world to create chaos, and at two years old, is well on her way to ending up famous or infamous—not sure which yet.

It's all a question as to whether or not she will use her genius for good or evil.

"Four kids is a lot for someone who normally only has

one." Cher bites her lip and watches our children descend on Mallory's playroom.

"Cher, baby, it's okay." I rub circles on her back, letting my hand slowly slide down to cup her round ass. My fingernails scrape across the denim seam between her legs, sending vibrations along her pussy lips. I know she feels it by the way her back tenses, and she slides a surreptitious glance my way.

We're on our way out of town for our five year anniversary, and I can't wait to get her naked in our private hot spring tub. Don't get me wrong, I love my children and my gloriously hectic life—but fuck, I miss the freedom of bending my wife over without interruption.

And with three kids, there are always interruptions—no matter the hour.

The garage door opens and Kemp walks in with a half dozen bags in each hand. He tilts his chin in my direction and grins. "Ready for the big weekend?"

"More than ready?" I slide him a sly grin.

"Are you?" Cher says loudly over the din of children running into the room.

"Uncle Kemp!" Cari throws herself at his legs, her favorite uncle—and she has a whole K9 center full of men vying for that position. He dumps the bags on the counter and then swoops her up into his arms. Their daughter Mallory is closer to Johnnie's age, and the poor boy is outnumbered by them three to one, and they let him know it every chance they get.

"It'll be fine, Cher. Get your asses out of here." Kemp

hobbles toward us with Cari in his arms, Mallory wrapped around one leg, and Johnnie wrapped around the other.

"Yeah, baby." I lean in and place my lips against her ear, making sure my supersonic children can't hear the filthy things I'm about to say. "As soon as we're on the mountain pass, I'm finding a place to pull over to give you the first of many orgasms this weekend. I want you gushing on my fingers, my tongue, and then my cock before we go to bed tonight."

Her breath catches and eyes sparkle. "I guess we're going."

Mari grins devilishly and waggles her fingers in our direction. "Bye!"

Heading up the pass, I pull off at a lookout point overlooking a valley of treetops with the mountain range and a setting sun in the distance. I back the tailgate to the edge and park, opening Cher's door and taking her hand. "Come with me, baby."

I pop up the window on the back of my truck camper shell and lower the tailgate, spreading out the blanket I set back here before leaving the house. Cher sits down, her legs dangling over the edge.I gave us barely enough space for me to stand between her legs, the traffic on the mountain pass fast enough that even if they could see me —which they can't with the way I'm parked—they'd be moving to fast to clock what I'm about to do to my woman.

I run my hands up the outside of her hips and pull her ass forward, nestling my hardening cock between thighs. Cher spreads her legs, the heat from her pussy telling me she's as ready for our anniversary celebration to start as I am. "Care to make a wager, Cher?"

She moans softly as I rub my fingers between us. "What are you willing to lose, Vale?"

"To you?" I lean forward and nibble along her jaw up to her earlobe where I whisper in her ear. "Everything."

"That's going to be a problem." She smiles, her head falling back to offer me her throat as her back arches and her breasts push against my chest.

"Why?" I bite through her thin cotton shirt and lacy bra cups to tease her nipples. As always she responds perfectly to me, reminding me how much I love playing with my wife.

She threads her fingers through my hair and throws me a soft smile when I look up at her. "Because I already have everything you have to give, and you have every-thing I have to give—as long as we're together, we can't lose."

"Fuck, I love you, baby." I claim her lips, plunging my tongue into her mouth. Cher wraps her legs around my waist, pulling me tight, clutching the back of my shirt.

"I can't wait to get naked with you."

"Yeah, but the first stop for tonight is here, watching this sunset, while I play with your pussy and make you come on my fingers. Scoot your sexy ass back and unbutton your jeans."

Cher doesn't question me, immediately undoing her fly and scooting back until her legs are straight. I unlace her boots and pull off her jeans, covering her legs loosely with a flannel blanket. I sit next to her, leaning back on my elbow and bending forward to trail kisses over her soft belly and full breasts.

I love her body. Every curve and stretch mark earned by carrying my children, and loving our family. She is the sexiest thing I've ever known, and I feel this as much today as I did the first night I laid eyes on her.

Without my asking, she spreads her legs as I slip my fingers inside her panties. She hot and slick with arousal, primed to orgasm for me without delay.

"You are so fucking perfect for me." I growl, slipping my fingers inside her heat.

She mewls, tossing her head back and rolling her hips. "Sometimes I miss you."

"I'm here, baby. I'm always here."

"How is it possible—" she gasps as I press my thumb against her clit and pump two fingers in and out of her cunt. "Oh god, yes, Vale. I'm so close."

"Come for me baby, then you can complete that thought."

I claim her lips as her orgasm rips through her, her pussy pulsing around my fingers. Deepening our kiss, I pull her into my arms as her climax wanes, kissing her with all the love and devotion that pumps through my veins every day. "Perfect."

She smiles lazily and looks at me through lidded, sexually satisfied eyes. "How is it possible that it's been five years? I vividly recall every detail from the moment you walked into the bar. The butterflies started in my tummy before you walked through the door. Then you appeared wearing well-worn jeans and a tight T-shirt with a sexy smirk on your face. I knew the moment I saw you that I was going to have you, but I never dreamed it would be for a lifetime."

"It's you and me baby, forever." I suck my fingers into my mouth and then kiss her deeply, the sun disappearing behind the mountains and the temperature dropping ten degrees instantly. Cher shivers and I sit up, pulling her into my arms. "Let's get on the road. We have a hot spring tub, a bottle of Jameson, and nothing else to do but pleasure each other until Sunday afternoon."

Coming next: Kemp and Mari in Mine to Crave.

Most of my books take place in Spring City, Colorado and feature cameo appearances from characters in past / present / and sometimes future books from all of my series. Check out my website for a cross-over / series map.

Also by Kameron Claire

Want more **Witty** Tongues, **Wicked** Needs, & **Wild** Deeds?

Hollywood Lights (Pre-Order)

* Billionaire Romance *

Show Time (Securing Selyne)

Money Shot

Three Shot

Martini Shot

Long Shot

Veteran K9 Team

** Military Romance **

Mine to Cherish

Mine to Crave

Mine to Possess

Mine to Adore

Mine to Covet

Mine to Worship

Mine to Protect

Mine to Treasure

Hot Nights with the Boss

** Forbidden Office / Age-Gap Romances **

Dating the Boss

Flirting with the Boss

Teasing the Boss

Tempting the Boss

Rangers Football

** Sports Romance **

Play Action Fake

Quarterback Sneak

Personal Foul

Two-Point Conversion

Red Zone

Man to Man Coverage

Short Story Collections and Bundles

Animal Attraction 4-Story Collection

Vegas Nights 4-Story Collection

Last Stand Saloon 4-Story Collection

Instalove Bundle

Grayson Enterprises Series

Bedding the Boss

Enticing the Ex

Tempting the Teacher

Wedding the Widow

About the Author

USA Today Bestselling Author Kameron Claire writes stories with witty tongues, wicked needs, and wild deeds. Her books emphasize strong female leads and the protective alpha males who know how to love and support kick-ass, take-charge women. Many of her books contain military veterans, boss babes, gentle but dominant men, and goofy K9 hijinks.

Find her everywhere via linktr.ee/kameronclaire
Signed Paperbacks and discounted eBook bundles are available exclusively on her store
Subscribe to the Witty, Wicked & Wild community and read all her books online for as little as $5 a month.

DARK HEARTS

By Helen Glenister

A Prequel

Dark Hearts Series

Mightier Than the Sword UK Publications